The Great Hunger

The first one's for you, Dad.

First published in 1998 by Franklin Watts

This paperback edition published in 1999

Franklin Watts
96 Leonard Street
London EC2A 4XD

Franklin Watts Australia
14 Mars Road
Lane Cove
NSW 2066

Editor: Kyla Barber
Designer: Kirstie Billingham
Consultant: Margaret Ward, Research Fellow in History,
Bath Spa University College

A CIP catalogue record for this book
is available from the British Library.

ISBN   0 7496 3447 2 (pbk)
       0 7496 3095 7 (hbk)

Dewey Classification 941.5

Printed in Great Britain

The Great Hunger

by
Malachy Doyle

Illustrations by Greg Gormley

W

FRANKLIN WATTS
NEW YORK•LONDON•SYDNEY

1

The Big Night

"Come on, Maggie, we'll be late,"
shouted Art.

"Late for what?" said his sister, looking
up from playing with her doll.

"The Big Night, silly," said Art.
"Up at the crossroads."

How could she forget it was The Big
Night – the night before potato picking?
Wasn't it only an hour ago that John Joe
had come calling for their father, with the
pipes under his arm? Father had taken the
fiddle off the wall above the hearth,
shouted "I'll see you up there!"
and off he'd gone.

"Are you ready, children?" said their mother. "It's time we left."

Maggie said goodbye to the pig, and away she went, swinging on Mother's arm. Art helped Grandad up the lane and they all made their way to the crossroads.

By the time they arrived, just about everyone was there, talking or dancing. Maggie ran off to play with wee Bridget, Mother was chatting to her friends, and Art and Grandad stood at the front, toes tapping. Father's fingers were jumping so fast you could hardly see them, his right arm moving in long steady sweeps, and music was coming out of his fiddle that would set a dead dog to dancing.

With John Joe on the pipes and Dinny
Gallagher on the whistle, everyone knew
they were the best jigs and reels for miles
around.

"One day you'll be
playing like that,
young Art Ryan,"
said his grandad
next to him.

"Will I, Grandad?"
said Art. "Do you
think so?" It was
Art's dream to
play the fiddle, but
every time he asked
to learn his father
would only say,
"All in good
time, son. All
in good time."

When the band played 'The Walls of Limerick' Art's mother grabbed him to make a pair, and Maggie came up and asked Grandad if he'd like to dance.

"Ah no, love," he answered. "I'd be proud to take the floor with such a fine young lady, but I'm afraid my old bones are a bit stiff tonight."

So Maggie danced with Bridget, while Grandad puffed away happily on his pipe.

After that they played 'Ryan's Fiddle'.

"How did it get its name, Grandad?" asked Art.

"Sure, don't you know that?" answered the old man. "It's our tune, it is, the family tune. My own grandad made it up years ago, before he came up this way from Tipperary. Every firstborn son of the Ryans has been playing it since."

The music and dancing carried on through the long evening, till the sun was low in the western sky, the moon was on the rise, and the first stars were appearing.

"Come on, children," said their mother,

when she could see they were tired.
"It's time we were getting back. It'll be
dark soon."

"Ah, Mother, can't we stay a bit
longer?" said Art. "Please!"

"No, love," she answered, shaking her
head. "Your grandad's worn out, and you
two need your sleep. We've all got to be up
bright and early."

"Who says I'm worn out?" said
Grandad, smiling. "Sure, I'm just working
up to a wee dance myself. Come on,

Maggie, let's show them how it's done!"

But he was only joking, as usual.
They waved to their father,
who'd be there for a
good while yet, and
began the long
walk home,
watching the last
of the sun go
down over the
islands as they
went. Art took
Grandad by the
arm, and Mother
and Maggie
walked on ahead,
singing quietly
together. Every time
the old man had to stop for a rest,
Art would look back longingly.

"One day it'll be me up there playing 'Ryan's Fiddle', Grandad," he said dreamily.

"True enough, Art," said his grandad. "God willing."

And they whistled the family tune to the stars all the rest of the way home.

2

Potato Picking

"Wake up, love."

Art groaned and rolled over. He didn't want to wake up.

"Come on, you lazy lumps," called their mother. "Your father's out there already. It's potato picking, remember?"

Potato picking! Art's favourite time of
year. It was a back-breaking job, sure
enough, out in the fields from dawn to
dusk. But you didn't have to go to school
till every last one was lifted. And all the
hard work was worth it and more when you
had your first taste of new potatoes hot
from the pan melting in your mouth. New
Donegal potatoes and buttermilk – the best
meal in the world!

Art threw off the blanket and jumped up from the hearth. Maggie grabbed it and covered her face, trying to hide from the daylight.

"Oh no you don't, Maggie Ryan," said Art, pulling it away with a laugh. "If I'm getting up, you are too!"

His mother handed him a mug of milk and a potato left over from the night before. It was an old grey one, last year's crop.

It wasn't a patch on the ones they'd be eating before the day was done, but Art wolfed it down nevertheless. He'd need the energy for the long hard day ahead of them.

Suddenly his father burst in at the door, white-faced.

"What's the matter, Tom?" asked Mother, looking up from the washing.

His arms were covered in slime. A dreadful smell washed through the room from the open door behind him.

"It's the potatoes," said their father quietly. "They're rotten, every last one."

Mother dropped the wet clothes on the floor and dashed out to the field, with Art and Maggie close behind.

They scrabbled in the mud, all three of them, pulling the slimy stalks from the sodden ground.

And Father was right – every single potato had turned to a stinking mush.

The foul smell of disease was everywhere.

Art's father sat down on a rock and put his head in his hands.

"Dear God," said his mother.
"What are we going to do?"

Art looked up. All across the valley the
fields were dotted with their friends and
neighbours. Every one of them had been at
the dance the night before, every one of
them had got up bright and early to bring in
the crop, and Art knew that at that moment
every one of them was staring at disaster.
The men were cursing, the women were
praying and the children were crying.

"What'll we eat, Art?" said little
Maggie, pulling at his shirt. "If we've no
potatoes, what'll we eat?"

"I don't know, Maggie," said Art,
putting his arm around her. "I don't know."

3

Troubled Times

There were no new Donegal potatoes that year, only the last of the old grey lumpers. Luckily they'd had a good crop the year before, so there was enough for a couple of extra months, though they were old and tasteless from being stored in the pit for so long. The children thought they were disgusting, but they knew there was nothing else, so they didn't complain.

Grandad nearly stopped eating altogether. Mother would dish up as many for him as she did for the others, but he'd slip them over to Art or Maggie every time.

"Ah, sure, one a day's enough for an old fellow like me," he'd say. "It's them that are

growing that needs the most." Soon he took
to his bed, refusing to get up at all.

One morning when the children
woke up, Mother was standing
in the doorway watching
the lane, and there
was no sign of
Father. Or the pig.

He came back
that evening with
a big sack of
yellow meal
on his back.

"Where's he
gone, Father?" said
Maggie sadly. "Where's my lovely pig?"

"I had to sell him, love," said Father,
putting a hand gently on her shoulder as
she tried to hold back the tears.

He took Art to one side.

"I have to go away to find work, son," he told him. "I might be gone a long time, and you'll maybe have to do the planting without me, but I'll be back by harvest, if not before."

"But who'll look after Mother and Maggie and Grandad?" said Art.

"You will, Art. It's up to you to make sure they're all right while I'm gone. Can you do that?"

Art nodded. "I'll try," he said bravely.

Father looked over at Mother.

"I went up to the Big House and paid the rent for the year, so the landlord's agent won't come bothering you while I'm gone. And I've got enough money left over for you to buy seed potatoes when they come in, and for another sack of meal when this one's finished. They say the farms in Antrim weren't so badly hit, so I'm going there to see if there's any work. I'll send money as soon as I can.

"The only thing there's left to sell is the fiddle, but it'd break old Grandad's heart to see it go out of the family, so I'm leaving it here. You're to look after it, Art. If things get really bad, get the best price you can for it. Do you understand?"

"Yes, Father," said Art. "But won't you need it with you? What will you play?"

"Oh, don't worry about me, lad," said Father. "Dinny Gallagher's made me a whistle, so I'll be all right."

And he strode off down the lane a short while later with a pack on his back and the whistle between his lips, playing 'Ryan's Fiddle'.

4

Learning the Fiddle

Grandad was ill. He lay in bed all day
and hardly touched his food. He'd chew
on a potato skin while there were still some
left, but when they were gone, and all there
was to eat was watery porridge made from
the yellow meal, he refused to touch it.

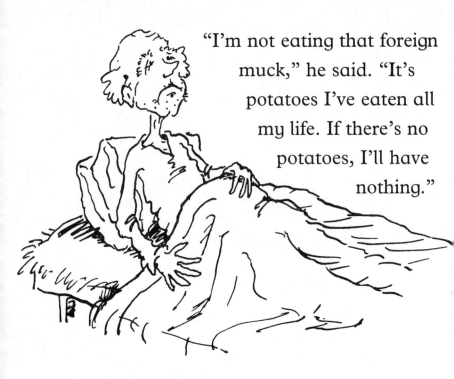

"I'm not eating that foreign muck," he said. "It's potatoes I've eaten all my life. If there's no potatoes, I'll have nothing."

Art couldn't bear to see him so sick and frail. He racked his brains to think of something to cheer him up. And then he spotted the fiddle, hanging above the hearth. Reaching it down, he pulled the bow across the strings.

"Tom, is that you? Are you back?" asked Grandad in a weak voice.

"No, it's only me, Grandad," said Art, and he played a few squeaky notes.

"Ah, it's a tonic to hear, though," said the old man. "Even if it sounds like there's a wee mouse stuck inside! Here, pass it over, Art, it's terrible out of tune."

Much to Art's surprise Grandad heaved himself up in his bed, took hold of the fiddle, and soon had it sorted out. He played a short burst of 'Ryan's Fiddle' before handing it back.

"Do you know what that one's called, young fellow?" he asked.

"Course I do, Grandad," said Art. "It's our tune!"

"Aye, it is too," said Grandad. "And it's about time you learnt to play it!"

From that day on, even though he still refused to eat more than the tiniest scrap of porridge, Grandad seemed to have a bit more energy. Every morning he'd give Art a lesson,

and in next to no time the boy was playing away as if he'd been born to it.

"It's in the blood!" said Grandad, clapping his hands. "You can tell you're a Ryan, and no mistaking."

He taught him 'The Trip to Sligo' so he could play a jig and 'The Hunter's Purse' so he knew a reel. Once Art had got the hang of it, he found he could play loads of tunes that he'd been carrying in his head without even knowing.

Art's mother could see how happy it made him, despite the hunger, so she decided to teach Maggie some of the old songs. The girl was missing her father,

and she needed cheering up. Maggie had
a sweet voice and learnt quickly, and
soon the cottage was full to bursting
every evening, for it was one of the few
left in the area where anyone had the
heart to make music.

5

The Second Harvest

Slowly but surely the time passed,
Art, Maggie and Mother planted the seed
potatoes, and the year of hunger moved
through its seasons.

They carried on as best they could,
though everyone missed Father sorely.

Then one night their prayers were
answered for in he walked, back in time
for harvest as he'd promised. He'd been so
worried about them, for the fever was all

around by now, and
he was amazed to
find a house full of
music, Maggie
singing a beautiful
tune, and Art
playing sweetly
on the fiddle.
He stood in the
doorway, unseen,
until the song was over, and
then entered, greeting everyone.
"My heart ached to be gone so long,"
he told them, hugging each in turn. "But
it's bursting with pride tonight – to see my
lovely wife, my own son on the fiddle and

my pretty wee girl singing like a lark. Sure, I'm a lucky man, even in these troubled times." Little Maggie snuggled in close to her father.

There were tears and laughter alike that night as Father told them stories of the places and people he'd seen on his travels. The family were overjoyed to be together once more, but they listened in horror to the news of disease and hunger stretching the length and breadth of Ireland.

Within a few days it felt as though
Father had never been away, and they all
settled back into the old routines. But their
happiness was not to last. Old age and the
long months of hunger finally caught up
with Grandad, and he died peacefully in
his sleep. It was Mother who found him.
Quietly she raised the children and they
gathered round his bedside to pray while
Father went to fetch the priest.

"It's a sad day," said the priest as they laid Grandad in the ground. "But he was a good man and he brought joy to those around him. It's a pity he had to go now, with his grandchildren so brave and so musical, and the potato plants strong and healthy in the fields. It's been a terrible year for everyone, but please God the worst is behind us."

"Aye, please God," whispered Art. Ever since he'd planted up the field he'd been having awful dreams about the coming harvest. But he'd kept them to himself, as he didn't want to worry the others.

They came from miles around to
Grandad's wake, everyone who was well
enough to travel. Songs were sung and
stories were told and they all remembered

him as a fine, hard-working man, with a great love for the fiddle and a constant twinkle in his eye.

It was a long night and there were a few sore heads after. But the morning was to bring far worse than headaches.

The next day was the start of potato picking, and Art and Maggie woke before anyone else, got dressed as quietly as mice, and went out to the fields.

The second they opened the door they knew. The foul small of decay hit them like a fist. Maggie burst into tears and ran back inside, but Art held his breath and

walked into the field. His worst nightmare had come true. The potato leaves had turned black and the whole crop was ruined once more.

6

The Long March

The following morning Father left for
Belfast.

"It's the only place I'm likely to find
decent work," he told them. "I'll send
money as soon as I can."

He'd have to. The last sack of meal

was almost empty. Unless he found a job they'd all starve, for there was nothing left to sell. Nothing but the fiddle.

The morning after he'd gone there was a loud banging on the door. It was the

landlord's agent. "I've come for your rent!" he demanded. Their mother gasped, and Art and Maggie came running to her side. "But it's not due yet! Can't you wait a week or two?" she pleaded. "My husband's gone to find work. He'll be sending money soon."

"That's what everyone says," said the man. "Lord Charlbury can't wait. He's closing up the Big House and going back to England. He says we're to evict anyone who won't pay."

"What does he mean, Mother?" asked Maggie when he'd gone. "What's going to happen?"

But Mother sat huddled over the fire, staring into the ashes, and wouldn't say a word to anyone.

The next morning the agent was back with a group of men. When he banged on the door Mother held her head in her hands and didn't move.

"Have you got the rent?" the agent asked when Art opened up. "It's your last chance." Art shook his head sadly.

"Then you'd better get outside. I'm under orders to tumble your cottage."

"Mother, Mother!" shouted Art, running back inside. "They're going to knock down the walls! We've got to get out, quick!"

He grabbed his mother with one hand and Maggie with the other and led them out. "Wait!" he yelled, as the men got ready. He ran back inside and grabbed the fiddle from above the fireplace. They stood and watched as the battering ram pounded their home to dust.

"I want Father," said
Maggie, between sobs.

"We'll find him," said Art, holding
her tight. "If we have to go all the way to
Belfast to do it."

"But how will we get there?" asked
little Maggie.

"We'll walk," said Art.

"And what will we eat?"

"Don't worry, Maggie," said Art,
though he had no idea. "I'll look after you."

And so began the long march to Belfast.

The roads were full of people – people in
rags, people with fever, people starving.
Most of them were heading for the towns,
where they thought there'd be food,
but Art kept to the back roads. He was

determined to avoid the fever, and his greatest fear was the workhouse. They'd take you in and feed you, all right, but he'd heard they'd split you up from your family. There was no way Art was going to let that happen.

They ate anything they could find – blackberries in the hedgerows, cabbage leaves from the fields, a fish from the river if they were  lucky. They stayed well away from the stinking potato fields where people scrabbled in the mud, eating whatever they could find, diseased or not.

NORTHSIDE CHRISTIAN COLLEGE

They slept in ditches, doorways and deserted farms. They passed piles of rubble where cottages had been tumbled, like their own.

Art knew they were heading in the right direction for Belfast, yet at the speed they were walking, and with his mother so ill  and weak – she was coughing badly and her skin looked grey – he wondered if they'd ever make it.

7

Belfast City

At long last they arrived in the city. They were amazed how busy it was. The streets were full of beggars, like everywhere else, but there were rich people too, going about their business as if there was nothing wrong with the world, and the

shop windows were packed with delights.

Art led them down to the docks, to see if they could find news of their father, but no one could help them. He was horrified to see cartloads of wheat, barley and oats being loaded on to ships. The carts were surrounded by soldiers, who were there to stop the starving people getting near.

"But this is Irish food!" Art shouted. "Don't send it away!"

"Aye, you tell them, lad," said an old woman next to him. "They won't listen to us."

"But I don't understand," said Art. "Why are they putting it on boats, when we're dying of hunger!"

"Well," said the woman. "They say it's

sold already, that's what they say. To people in other countries, people with money. Only the landlords can stop it, or the politicians. But they won't. They'd rather see us starve."

Art led Maggie and his mother back to the town centre and they set up home in the doorway of an empty shop. All day he and Maggie stood out in front, playing fiddle and singing. Most people walked straight past, but some tossed a few coins into Art's cap.

Each night they
went to the soup
kitchen in Linenhall
Street, where Art,
Maggie and their
mother would
have a hot bowl
of broth and
warm themselves
up before heading
back for another night in the doorway.

One afternoon, as the sun was shining
and Art was playing 'Ryan's Fiddle', an old
fellow pulled out a whistle and joined in.

"Where'd you learn our tune?" asked
Art when they'd finished.

"Oh, I heard it from a friend of mine
called Tom," said the beggar. "We
worked on a farm together up the coast
last summer."

"Tom Ryan?" said Art. "That's my father! We've been looking for him for ages! Do you know where he is?"

"Funny enough," said the man, "I saw him just a couple of weeks ago. He was looking for work, like everyone else. Told me he was off to Liverpool to see if there was any there."

Art went down to the harbour straight away to find out how much it would cost to go over the sea.

It was only a few shillings. With a bit more busking they'd have enough.

"Thank God," said Mother, smiling weakly when Art told her where Father was, and that they were going there to find him. "Maybe our luck's turning at last".

TURNER AMERICA

TAPSCOTT'S
BELFAST
LIVERPOOL
DIRECT
T.EIRSHIP
NGUARD

And it was. Art and Maggie scraped together enough money for the tickets, and a few mornings later they boarded the boat.

As it pulled away from the quay Maggie and her mother stood on deck, waving farewell to Ireland, with Art in between them, fiddle in hand. The tune of 'Ryan's Fiddle' joined the cry of the seagulls, at the end of one life and the beginning of another.

The Potato Famine

Life in Ireland before the Famine

In the early nineteenth century many Irish people, especially in the West, lived on tiny farms which they rented from landlords (many of whom were English). But they were generally well fed, healthy and warm, for there was a ready supply of turf to burn on the fire. They ate almost nothing but potatoes as these were cheap and easy to grow. Potatoes needed little work and the long winter months were spent talking, making music and telling stories.

Most of the country people lived in simple cabins with just a single room with no windows. They had very little furniture, and a pig often slept in the corner.

Potato Blight

In 1845 a blight, or disease, rotted the potatoes, ruining the crop in many areas. The people had little else to eat and soon became desperate. They sold everything they owned to buy food, but most went hungry and many were forced to eat the seed potatoes they should have planted the following year. The blight came back in 1846, and the complete potato crop failed. There was no food left and people began to die in their thousands. In 1847 the plants were healthy, but not enough seeds had been sewn, and it was followed by two more terrible years of blight.

At the start of the famine almost nine million people lived in Ireland. By the end, over one million had died of hunger and disease, and another million had emigrated to Britain or America. A further million emigrated over the following five years.

Government and the Landlords

The Government
in London, which
controlled all of
Great Britain and
Ireland, was very
slow to realise
how bad things
were, and did
little to help
the starving.
There were
many other
crops growing
in Ireland, but most
of them were exported
overseas, and nothing
was done to stop this.

In time the Government brought in Indian
corn, which was ground into yellow meal, but it
was not enough to stop great numbers of Irish
people starving to death.

Some landlords helped their tenants, but many did nothing. The worst ones evicted families who could not pay their rent and pulled down their homes to stop them returning.

Workhouses were built at this time for people without homes. They separated men from women and children from parents. Once inside, many people suffered worse disease and hunger than those queueing up to get in.

Irish Traditional Music

The folk music of Ireland is famous throughout the world. The violin, or fiddle, is the main instrument. The uilleann (elbow) pipes are a form of bagpipe. The whistle is a simple instrument that would now be made of metal, but when this story is set people would probably have played home-made wooden ones. Traditional musicians often made up their own tunes, which were then named after them.

Sparks: Historical Adventures

ANCIENT GREECE
The Great Horse of Troy – The Trojan War
0 7496 3369 7 (hbk)   0 7496 3538 X (pbk)
The Winner's Wreath – Ancient Greek Olympics
0 7496 3368 9 (hbk)   0 7496 3555 X (pbk)

INVADERS AND SETTLERS
Boudicca Strikes Back – The Romans in Britain
0 7496 3366 2 (hbk)   0 7496 3546 0 (pbk)
Viking Raiders – A Norse Attack
0 7496 3089 2 (hbk)   0 7496 3457 X (pbk)
Erik's New Home – A Viking Town
0 7496 3367 0 (hbk)   0 7496 3552 5 (pbk)
TALES OF THE ROWDY ROMANS
The Great Necklace Hunt
0 7496 2221 0 (hbk)   0 7496 2628 3 (pbk)
The Lost Legionary
0 7496 2222 9 (hbk)   0 7496 2629 1 (pbk)
The Guard Dog Geese
0 7496 2331 4 (hbk)   0 7496 2630 5 (pbk)
A Runaway Donkey
0 7496 2332 2 (hbk)   0 7496 2631 3 (pbk)

TUDORS AND STUARTS
Captain Drake's Orders – The Armada
0 7496 2556 2 (hbk)   0 7496 3121 X (pbk)
London's Burning – The Great Fire of London
0 7496 2557 0 (hbk)   0 7496 3122 8 (pbk)
Mystery at the Globe – Shakespeare's Theatre
0 7496 3096 5 (hbk)   0 7496 3449 9 (pbk)
Plague! – A Tudor Epidemic
0 7496 3365 4 (hbk)   0 7496 3556 8 (pbk)
Stranger in the Glen – Rob Roy
0 7496 2586 4 (hbk)   0 7496 3123 6 (pbk)
A Dream of Danger – The Massacre of Glencoe
0 7496 2587 2 (hbk)   0 7496 3124 4 (pbk)
A Queen's Promise – Mary Queen of Scots
0 7496 2589 9 (hbk)   0 7496 3125 2 (pbk)
Over the Sea to Skye – Bonnie Prince Charlie
0 7496 2588 0 (hbk)   0 7496 3126 0 (pbk)
TALES OF A TUDOR TEARAWAY
A Pig Called Henry
0 7496 2204 0 (hbk)   0 7496 2625 9 (pbk)
A Horse Called Deathblow
0 7496 2205 9 (hbk)   0 7496 2624 0 (pbk)
Dancing for Captain Drake
0 7496 2234 2 (hbk)   0 7496 2626 7 (pbk)
Birthdays are a Serious Business
0 7496 2235 0 (hbk)   0 7496 2627 5 (pbk)

VICTORIAN ERA
The Runaway Slave – The British Slave Trade
0 7496 3093 0 (hbk)   0 7496 3456 1 (pbk)
The Sewer Sleuth – Victorian Cholera
0 7496 2590 2 (hbk)   0 7496 3128 7 (pbk)
Convict! – Criminals Sent to Australia
0 7496 2591 0 (hbk)   0 7496 3129 5 (pbk)
An Indian Adventure – Victorian India
0 7496 3090 6 (hbk)   0 7496 3451 0 (pbk)
Farewell to Ireland – Emigration to America
0 7496 3094 9 (hbk)   0 7496 3448 0 (pbk)
The Great Hunger – Famine in Ireland
0 7496 3095 7 (hbk)   0 7496 3447 2 (pbk)
Fire Down the Pit – A Welsh Mining Disaster
0 7496 3091 4 (hbk)   0 7496 3450 2 (pbk)
Tunnel Rescue – The Great Western Railway
0 7496 3353 0 (hbk)   0 7496 3537 1 (pbk)
Kidnap on the Canal – Victorian Waterways
0 7496 3352 2 (hbk)   0 7496 3540 1 (pbk)
Dr. Barnardo's Boys – Victorian Charity
0 7496 3358 1 (hbk)   0 7496 3541 X (pbk)
The Iron Ship – Brunel's Great Britain
0 7496 3355 7 (hbk)   0 7496 3543 6 (pbk)
Bodies for Sale – Victorian Tomb-Robbers
0 7496 3364 6 (hbk)   0 7496 3539 8 (pbk)
Penny Post Boy – The Victorian Postal Service
0 7496 3362 X (hbk)   0 7496 3544 4 (pbk)
The Canal Diggers – The Manchester Ship Canal
0 7496 3356 5 (hbk)   0 7496 3545 2 (pbk)
The Tay Bridge Tragedy – A Victorian Disaster
0 7496 3354 9 (hbk)   0 7496 3547 9 (pbk)
Stop, Thief! – The Victorian Police
0 7496 3359 X (hbk)   0 7496 3548 7 (pbk)
Miss Buss and Miss Beale – Victorian Schools
0 7496 3360 3 (hbk)   0 7496 3549 5 (pbk)
Chimney Charlie – Victorian Chimney Sweeps
0 7496 3351 4 (hbk)   0 7496 3551 7 (pbk)
Down the Drain – Victorian Sewers
0 7496 3357 3 (hbk)   0 7496 3550 9 (pbk)
The Ideal Home – A Victorian New Town
0 7496 3361 1 (hbk)   0 7496 3553 3 (pbk)
Stage Struck – Victorian Music Hall
0 7496 3363 8 (hbk)   0 7496 3554 1 (pbk)
TRAVELS OF A YOUNG VICTORIAN
The Golden Key
0 7496 2360 8 (hbk)   0 7496 2632 1 (pbk)
Poppy's Big Push
0 7496 2361 6 (hbk)   0 7496 2633 X (pbk)
Poppy's Secret
0 7496 2374 8 (hbk)   0 7496 2634 8 (pbk)
The Lost Treasure
0 7496 2375 6 (hbk)   0 7496 2635 6 (pbk)

20th-CENTURY HISTORY
Fight for the Vote – The Suffragettes
0 7496 3092 2 (hbk)   0 7496 3452 9 (pbk)
The Road to London – The Jarrow March
0 7496 2609 7 (hbk)   0 7496 3132 5 (pbk)
The Sandbag Secret – The Blitz
0 7496 2608 9 (hbk)   0 7496 3133 3 (pbk)
Sid's War – Evacuation
0 7496 3209 7 (hbk)   0 7496 3445 6 (pbk)
D-Day! – Wartime Adventure
0 7496 3208 9 (hbk)   0 7496 3446 4 (pbk)
The Prisoner – A Prisoner of War
0 7496 3212 7 (hbk)   0 7496 3455 3 (pbk)
Escape from Germany – Wartime Refugees
0 7496 3211 9 (hbk)   0 7496 3454 5 (pbk)
Flying Bombs – Wartime Bomb Disposal
0 7496 3210 0 (hbk)   0 7496 3453 7 (pbk)
12,000 Miles From Home – Sent to Australia
0 7496 3370 0 (hbk)   0 7496 3542 8 (pbk)